W9-BTG-205

Anklet and Other Stories

Anklet and Other Stories

by

Shome Dasgupta

Golden Antelope Press
715 E. McPherson
Kirksville, Missouri 63501
2017

Copyright ©2017 by Shome Dasgupta
Story Images Copyright ©2017 by Indira Kalyan Dutta
Cover Design by Russell Nelson

All rights reserved. No portion of this publication may be
duplicated in any way without the expressed written con-
sent of the publisher, except in the form of brief excerpts
or quotations for review purposes.

ISBN   978-1-936135-31-8 (1-936135-31-0)

Library of Congress Control Number: 2017941692

Published by:
Golden Antelope Press
715 E. McPherson
Kirksville, Missouri 63501

Available at:
Golden Antelope Press
715 E. McPherson
Kirksville, Missouri, 63501
Phone: (660) 665-0273
http://www.goldenantelope.com
Email: ndelmoni@gmail.com

In Memory of Angelique

Acknowledgments:

Indira Kalyan Dutta created the delightful sketches that go with the stories: "The Boatman's Home," "Samosa," "This is My Head," and "Tagore's Kiss" (on pages 3, 26, 37, and 52).

- "The Boatman's Home" appeared in *Café Irreal*.
- "The Bullies" appeared in an alternate version in *Necessary Fiction*.
- "1-0" appeared in *Verdad Magazine*.
- "Anklet" appeared in *The Kartika Review*.
- "Samosa" appeared in *The Ranfurly Review*.
- "This Is My Head" appeared in *The Coachella Review*.
- "Tagore's Kiss" appeared in *Two Hawks Quarterly*.
- "Empty Chair" appeared in *Gertrude Press*.

Contents

The Boatman's Home

The man rowed the boat along the Ganges River; the mosquitoes were still menacing. The sun was half gone— falling below either the horizon or a thin line of smog. The cooler temperature brought the people out to the banks of the river. Children threw mud at each other and then they cleaned themselves using the river as their tub, as their parents, cousins, or older siblings screamed at them for playing with the filthy globs of wet dirt. A few women washed clothes and scrubbed their shirts against large rocks and tin plates while their half-naked husbands stood on the banks and scoured themselves until a fresh layer of skin appeared. Others prayed and threw marigolds into the Ganges, and watched them drift away to the Bay Of Bengal, where mounds and mounds of marigolds had probably formed some kind of dam from their prayers and wishes.

The boat was small and narrow; the wood was chipping—there were holes, and only a few of them were patched. It made a creaking sound as we made our way down the brown river and rocked side to side. The rickety pieces of wood seemed to be cautious and grateful that the river did not swallow the boat as it snuck softly along the surface. The rower, however, did not seem to exert extra energy to keep the boat traveling forward. He wore a tight white shirt and a blue dhoti. He wore no shoes, and his legs looked like the thin pieces of wood that kept the wobbly boat together. Except for his arms and back, his body seemed meatless. His biceps bulged in each row, and I could see the muscles of his back tighten with energy as he swung his arm back and forward. He had gray hair and gray stubble on his face. There was only room for one person to sit in the boat. I sat while he stood and paddled. He had not said a word to me nor had he looked at me since I sat down.

"Nice today," I said.

"Yes," the man replied.

I did not think he even moved his lips, but he somehow managed to speak. After he paddled about five more times I spoke again.

"So. How long have you been a boatman?"

He replied without even thinking. It was as if he knew my question before I asked it.

"Forty-five years."

"You don't get tired of it?" I asked. "You've must have been pretty young when you started."

"I have no choice," he said. "My burden came when I was a child, and since then, I have carried the weight of the river upon my shoulders."

"Why did you start so young?" I asked.

He spat into the water. He still had not looked at me all this while.

"I just came to take a voyage on the river," he said.

He did not look like he was going to say anything else. He wanted to end the conversation there.

"And then what?" I asked.

"I was a child taking a trip on the Ganges," the man said. "I stole some money from a dog's mouth. I was not sure how the dog came upon the money, and if it was taking the cash to his owner, but I took it nonetheless. The dog did not care though. He went walking along the street as I am sure he would always do every day."

He stopped talking, and again I had to ask him what happened next. He still had not looked at me.

"Well," the man said. "I used the money to pay the boatman so that he could show me where the river leads. He told me that I shouldn't. I asked him why, and he said because it leads to pain. I insisted on going, and the boatman took my money, and I sat in the boat as he rowed."

"And then what?" I asked. "What did the man look like?"

"Oh, he was old," the man replied. "He looked like he hadn't eaten in years. His eyes were dark red, and he only had a few teeth left."

The man paddled a few more times without saying anything. I was not sure if that was the end of his story, so I asked him again to continue.

"Well," he said. "There is not much after that."

The man stopped talking. He looked down the river and took a deep breath. I did not have to ask him to continue though.

"He never answered," the man said.

"What do you mean?" I asked.

"The boatman never answered," he replied.

"Well what happened?" I asked.

"He tied a brick to his leg and jumped into the river,"

the man said. "He drowned. His decayed matter is probably still floating around."

"I can't believe it," I said.

"After he jumped," the man said. "I picked up the oars and paddled my way back to my home. But people along the banks kept asking for rides, and so I gave them what they wanted. For forty-five years I have yet to see my home. I cannot go back. This river pulls me in as the sun pulls the earth."

"Amazing," I said.

We both stopped talking. I could not believe that such a thing had happened to him. The Ganges seemed to have some kind of power over him. As the boatman rowed, I noticed that he was in complete harmony with the river. Each stroke caused gentle ripples and made a quiet, peaceful whirring noise that could almost lull me to sleep. He closed his eyes from time to time, and the motion of his arms became his tool of vision. I wondered how many times the man had rowed this boat up and down the Ganges River, for he seemed to be like a fish in total synchrony with the river's current. But with each stroke, he winced slightly. He had become one of Hades' citizens.

As he rowed, and as we remained silent, I continued to observe the Ganges' banks. It was almost dark, and most of the river dwellers had gone back to their homes to eat fish and rice. A few people were still in the river washing themselves, praying, or urinating. Candles with flickering light could be seen inside some houses, and the blackbirds had ceased their cawing in hope of spare fish, banana peels, and bread thrown out after dinner. They would have to compete with the gangly stray cats and red-eyed dogs for their meals. Somewhere in the midst of a cloud of pollution and people, coming from behind the row of houses set on the banks of the river, conches could be heard, blowing to let everyone know about night's arrival.

The man stopped rowing and placed the oars on the floor of the boat. He stretched his back and his legs. He closed his eyes for a few seconds, and then he looked at me.

"Anyway," the man said. "Where are you from?"

"I live in Chennai," I replied. "I came to feel the Ganges."

The man smiled.

"You will never see your home," he said.

He picked up a cement block that was tied to his leg and jumped into the river. The boat rocked side to side, and the water splashed me as he dove into the river. I looked for him through the water, but it was too dark to see. The river had seeped into his blood, into his immune system like a virus, and he had succumbed to its force. He had, finally, given in to his master so that he could be free of it. I shivered as the murky water dripped from my head onto my neck. I picked up the oars to row back to where we had come from. On my way back, I saw a silhouette of a man. He held a candle in his hand and it flickered as he waved it and motioned me to go to him. The man was old and held a cane in his other hand. He climbed onto the boat, blew his candle out, and mumbled something. All that I could make out was that he wanted a ride.

1-0

I left Landmark Bookstore and walked lazily along Lord Sinha Road. After browsing the bookstore, I had decided to take a walk. The street was crowded with cars and pedestrians on the Saturday afternoon. I thought about buying some peanuts, but then decided to purchase a container on the way back, for the store looked extremely busy with customers. I realized that in any store in Kolkata, the customers always took a long time to buy the things they wanted, and sometimes, they would take a long time and then not buy anything. From the smallest of stores, like a peanut store, to large clothing companies, the customers would occupy the employees' attention for as long as a half hour to forty-five minutes. Many times, they would have multiple employees helping them. Once I waited for about twenty minutes to buy a couple of pastries, because the customer ahead of me kept asking the merchant questions, and then would talk to the group of friends that surrounded him. He finally bought one small sweet and left. If I were back in Lafayette, or anywhere else in America, I normally would get agitated. Sometimes, I would walk out of the store and go to a different one, or I would pout and sigh loudly. My tolerance for waiting was not too great in America. For some reason, in Kolkata, my length of patience increased. I was glad to observe this in myself, and hoped that it would remain with me when I went back to America.

The pollution was thick on that Saturday afternoon. The small huts had already begun to make their foods for dinner, and this caused even more smoke to appear, as the clouds from the primitive ovens and stoves drifted onto the street. Several children ran around and played, and several adults stood on the sidewalk and talked and laughed loudly. Others briskly walked towards their destinations. I had become accustomed to the honking and other loud traffic noises, the vehicles without mufflers or catalytic converters, and I barely noticed their sounds anymore. On the other side of the road was a long wall or barrier, which I guessed separated the city traffic from a neighborhood. Peering over the wall were huge, fulsome trees. I walked over and stood underneath the shade and rested from the heat of the sun before I made my way back to the peanut store.

As I wiped the sweat off my face with the sleeve of my shirt, I felt a hard knock against the back of my head. It stung, and I flinched in reaction. I looked to the ground to see what hit me and saw a dead blackbird on the sidewalk. It was bloody and half chewed or mangled. I immediately panicked and rubbed the back of my head as I made moaning noises. I looked at my hand and saw blood, but I was not sure whether the blood came from the dead bird or my head. I looked around and no one else seemed to have noticed what happened. Pacing back and forth, I did not know what to do. All kinds of illnesses could occur from such a cut. As I felt around my head, I could not feel any kind of open wound, and realized that the blood came from the blackbird. I sighed loudly and stared at it. The beak was half gone, its eyes were pecked, and most of its feathers were lost. I assumed it had been in a fight with some kind of other animal- most probably a Kolkatan cat.

As I turned around, a man dressed in a black suit stood before me. He wore a maroon scarf and a cricketer's hat. He had a thin and neatly trimmed mustache and very dark skin, which made the whites of his eyes stare directly at me.

"Hello," I said.

The man spoke in Bengali, and I could not understand most of the words he said.

"English," I said.

He smile and played with the scarf around his neck. His teeth were bright white and were perfect.

"Yes," he said. "You were hit by the blackbird."

"You saw that?" I asked. "It really scared me."

He laughed loudly and placed his hands in his pockets.

"Where are you from?" he asked.

"I live in America, but my family is from here," I replied.

"Yes," he said. "You were hit by the blackbird. I saw it."

"Yes," I said. "It really scared me. I just need to wash my head, and I think everything should be okay."

The man laughed and placed one of his hands on each end of the scarf, as someone would do to choke another person.

"Come," the man said. "Wash your hair at my place.

Nearby."

"Oh," I said. "I'll just wait until I go home. I should be getting back actually. We'll be eating dinner soon."

"Yes," the man said. "Come. Come. Follow me."

He tugged my arm and motioned me to follow him. He was a few inches taller than me and very thin. He wore white tennis shoes, and his footsteps gently tapped the ground as he walked. I did not know what compelled me to follow him, but I did. I really wanted to wash the blood from my hair before I went back to the flat for dinner. Just the thought of a dead bird's blood in my hair made me feel uncomfortable let alone actually having the blood in my hair.

I noticed that as we walked along Lord Sinha Road, the other people on the street looked at us, or to be more specific, they stared at me. The pedestrians who stood on the same side of the street as us, moved aside as we walked, which was something I had never seen while walking the streets of Kolkata. Normally, no one would move aside to let other walkers pass. They looked at me, they looked at my clothes, and they appeared to be afraid. No one made eye contact with the man I followed, but they stared into the ground or glanced at me. I looked at them and noticed that they all had small indentions or some kind of mark imprinted on their foreheads. They looked like three or four small lines in the shape of a paw or some kind of animal's foot. I began to have doubts about the whole situation, and started to think that I should go back to the driver and go to the flat. I stopped walking.

"Hey," I said.

The man stopped and turned around. He motioned me

to follow him.

"I think I'll just go home," I said.

A small crowd of people surrounded us.

"Come," he said. "Wash your hair here."

He pointed to a gate, which led to a large courtyard and a house. The crowd of people were completely silent. I smiled at some of them and said hello, but everyone stood expressionless. The man in the black suit tugged my arm and walked towards the gate. I followed him, and the people began to walk away slowly. Some walked backwards and continued to look at me, while others kept turning around to see what was happening. The man opened the gate and smiled. He lifted his arm to let me in first.

"Come," he said. "The blackbird's blood."

The floor of the courtyard consisted of granite or marble. There were a few wrought iron tables and chairs. The furniture surrounded a small pond where fish swam. On the outer edges of the courtyard were large bushes that came to about my chin. The house was huge. The patio consisted of more marble or granite flooring, and there were two pillars that held up the porch's roof. The façade was dark red and looked about two stories high. I had never seen such a big house before, for most of my friends and relatives lived in flats or smaller houses. An old lady dressed in a red and black sari sat on a rocking chair on the patio. She rocked back and forth and watched us as we moved towards the door of the house.

"Hello," I said.

She smiled and continued to rock the chair. I noticed that she wore bright white tennis shoes. The man did not say a word to her, nor did she say anything to the man.

Her hair was black and gray and tightly parted in the middle. When she smiled, I saw a set of crooked and black teeth along with black gums. The man opened the door and told me to follow him.

"Come," he said. "The washroom is on the right."

I followed him into the washroom which, again, consisted of marble or granite. He handed me a towel and left the washroom. I closed the door, rinsed my hair, and saw tiny streams of blood flowing into the drain. I rubbed some soap on the back of my head and then rinsed it again until I was sure all the blood was gone. I looked through the washroom window and saw in a yard, a badminton net and a line of clothes that had been hung to dry. The man's face appeared directly in front of the window, just like a head shot would be shown on a television commercial. He smiled.

"Come," he said. "Play badminton."

He held up a wooden racket. The frame was pretty thick, and it looked like an old tennis racket. I walked outside to the side of the house where the man stood. He handed me a racket similar to his and smiled.

"I really should be going," I said.

"One game," the man replied.

He walked to one side of the net where a large wooden bucket rested on a small table. I walked to the other side of the net. I had only played the game a few times, and I assumed that the man in the black suit was a good badminton player. He turned around, with the smile still woven into his face, and placed the birdie behind his back.

"Ready," he said.

I nodded. He quickly served the birdie, which was

black, and it barely made it over the net. I ran to the net and hit the birdie back over the net. I had never seen such a birdie before, but I guessed that, since he probably played a lot, he used a special brand. The man sprinted to the edge of the yard and hit it over the net again. I was able to return it, but I had it too high, and this gave the man the time to prepare for his hit, and he used all his might. I could barely see the thing because he hit it too quickly, and it smacked me right in my forehead. Stunned by the hit, I stumbled and fell, which caused the man to laugh. I could also hear the old lady who sat on the porch laugh as well. I stood and brushed the dirt off my pants and checked my elbows for any blood or scrapes. The man continued to laugh as I rubbed my forehead to lessen the stinging sensation. Angry and frustrated, I wanted to hit him in the face with the birdie as well, so I decided to play another point. I looked for the birdie, and saw it a few steps ahead of me. As I walked towards it, I screamed and rubbed my forehead again. We were playing badminton with a dead blackbird, similar to the one that hit me on the back of the head. The man continued to laugh. I ran to the washroom and cleaned my face and hands. I began to cry as well as I was frightened by this experience. I ran back into the yard where the man stood next to the large wooden bucket.

"You're sick," I shouted. "What do you think you're doing? Are you crazy?"

The happy expression on his face quickly dissolved to a worried look.

"What is wrong with you?" I asked.

The man did not say anything, but he stuck out his

hand to shake mine; but I refused to respond. Then he tried to place his hand on my shoulder, but I pushed it away. He looked sad.

"Badminton," he said.

"Shut up," I replied.

I walked past the porch, where the old lady ate mango on her rocking chair, to the gates at the front of the court-yard. Outside were a small group of people. They seemed to have been waiting for me. The crowd looked at me curiously and kept staring at my forehead. They all had some kind of scar or imprint on their forehead, and as I felt the top of my face, I realized that I had one as well. I quickly ran back to the Landmark Bookstore, where the driver waited for me. I entered into the back seat and told him to go back to the flat. He looked at me in the rearview mirror, smiled, and then laughed.

"Badminton," he said.

During the drive back I had to think of an excuse to tell my parents and grandmother. I was sure they were going to ask me what had happened. I decided to tell them that I stumbled and fell on some rocks.

Anklet

You stand there by yourself. I want to be with you, Stranger.
Together, we will be alone.
Away.

I stood on the banks of the Ganges as it passed through Kolkata. To my right was a family bathing in the river: the boy and the girl splashed each other and shouted and laughed, and the mother and father wiped themselves with towels. I took off my shoes and socks, and went into the water where it just came to my ankles. The sun was mostly down, and a breeze came with the current of the river. I looked around and couldn't see anyone else—I could only see the river's infinity. The two children, while chasing each other, ran into me, and I fell over—immersed in the Ganges. I swallowed some of the water and tasted Kolkata. I couldn't really explain it. It was a mixture of dirt and spirituality. I stood up and coughed, and the parents came over and apologized, making sure that I was okay. The children laughed and ran away.

"Sorry," the man said. "These children know no boundaries."

His skin was as dark as the river, and he was thin—his ribs pushed against the inside of his skin. He had dark black hair which was partially covered with soap suds, and a thin mustache. They must live in one of the nearby huts.

"Are you okay?" the woman asked.

Take me away. I love my brother. I love his children. I do not love myself. Take me away with you. Your brown eyes. That scruff on your chin. I will lick you up. Together, we will be free.

She was beautiful. She was skinny, but unlike her husband, she had enough flesh to hide any sight of her ribs. Her hair came down to the middle of her back, and her skin color reminded me of the perfect cup of tea and cream I had earlier that day. I coughed a few more times and nodded my head.

"I'm fine," I replied.

"Come," the man said. "Dry yourself. I have a towel."

I followed the man and the woman to their house which was just set off the river. It was a small wooden hut—I could see the different sizes and types of wooden boards used to make the door, the house. It was a one room place. The floor, or ground, consisted of patches of dirt and wood and brick. The door was kept open to let the breeze pass through. The lady gave me a towel. She wrapped a small piece of a maroon cloth around her body. She looked more beautiful than when she was naked. The subtle hints of what lay underneath the small cloth, her black eyes, and her long black hair could have easily made her a siren in Homer's epic poem. She didn't even have to sing.

Look at me. Look at me as you do. I know. You see beauty, but I am just dirt and water. I am mud everywhere. Clean me. Wash me. Lick me. I love everyone, but myself. Take me away.

The man wore a white cloth around his hip and a sleeveless white shirt. He apologized again for the mishap. "No problem," I said.

"Here," the lady said. "I'll help."

She took the towel from my hands and dried my face, hair, and neck.

"Please," she said. "Take your clothes off. You will become sick."

Strip yourself of everything. And I will too. Together we will go away on the Ganges. Forever and ever we will go. Can you hear what I am thinking? Can you see the way I am looking at you? Dear Stranger, my Nothing. Hear me, please. Take me away.

"I'll be okay."

"I'll give you some of Kumar's clothes," she said. "And when your clothes dry, you can change again."

Kumar went outside and told the children to come in because it was becoming dark. The woman handed me pants and a white t-shirt.

"It is similar to what you are wearing now," she replied.

"What is your name?" I asked.

I am yours. This is my name. We are each other.

"Shivaa," she said.

Destroy me. Make me crumble.

The children laughingly ran into the house followed by Kumar.

"We are eating fish for dinner," he said. "Please sit and eat with us."

"Please," I said. "I don't want to be a bother. I'll make my way out now."

"Please," Shivaa said. "Eat with us. We never have company. Have some fish while your clothes dry, and then make your way out."

Stay, please. You will like my cooking. I did not know it until now, but I cooked for you. Taste it. Breathe it. As I want to breathe you.

I agreed to their suggestion. Kumar set the table—a small wooden one with uneven legs.

"Can I help with anything?" I asked.

"No," he said. "No. Please sit and stay warm."

I sat on a wobbly wooden chair that had a cushion. The pillow had patterns of circles, squares, and triangles in reds, greens, and blues.

"I made that pillow," Shivaa said.

Rest your head upon my pillow.

"Pretty," I said.

She went to the middle of the room and drew the curtain, which was attached to a clothesline, going from one end of the room to the other—serving as a wall. I could see her silhouette as she changed her clothes. I could not

help but to imagine her nipples, trying hard to burn holes
through the curtain with my eyes.

Are you watching me? A naked ghost, waiting to moan.

When she came out she wore a long white gown which
was transparent enough to see the brown of her body. I
wanted to kiss her. I went outside and smoked a cigarette,
and by the time I was finished, the fish was ready.

"Let us eat," Kumar said.

He put the fish on a large plate. Shivaa put a bowl of
rice and a bowl of vegetables on the table.

"It is not much," she said.

"It's more than enough," I replied.

The children sat around the table, and I squeezed in at
one of the corners.

"So how long have you all been living here?" I asked.

*I have never lived here. Not now. Not before. Not after. I
am always gone.*

"All our lives," Kumar said. "After the death of our
parents, we took over the house. It has come a long way,
but still needs more work."

"Your parents?" I asked.

"Yes," he said. "Shivaa and I are siblings. I, three years
older."

I speedily ate my food.

"I will leave you my contact information," I said. "Call
me and I will be happy to help you out."

Help.

"I am sorry," Kumar said. "I cannot accept the offer for I do not have the money to pay for such services."

"Please," I said. "At no cost. Or this wonderful dinner will be my pay."

They were excited by my response and immediately offered me more food, and I graciously accepted it. As we talked, I found out more about them: Kumar was a fisherman and Shivaa took care of the house and sometimes helped out with her brother's work. They didn't have enough money to provide schooling for the children, but the sister made an effort to teach them the basics.

"It is enough for them to survive," she said.

I want to survive with you. Teach me. Free me. I love them. I love them all. But the door is too small. The river, too big.

I told them some general things about myself–that I lived in America and was visiting my relatives in Kolkata. They told me more about themselves.

The children didn't belong to the brother or the sister, but to another brother who couldn't be found. They weren't sure if he was dead, but they hadn't heard from him in three years. The siblings, collectively, decided to take care of the children, and neither of them had been married before. As we ate our dinner, my attraction to Shivaa increased. She had a human quality that I could not describe–a certain gentleness. Perhaps I found something spiritual in her.

I read your mind, Stranger, Friend. Do it. And when it is all done, I will be gone.

The evening breeze that I had felt while standing in the Ganges must have been a sign of a storm coming. As we finished dinner, I heard thunder and saw flashes of lightning through the window. The black sky was framed with bright bolts, surrounded with crashing sounds. The rain poured hard. The children weren't scared; however, my emotions were quite the opposite.

"I should go before it gets any worse," I said.

Not yet. It is not the time. Not now. But soon.

"No," Kumar said. "You must not in this weather. Please stay. The storm should be here for a while, and then who knows what will happen to the electricity—and then the traffic will be horrible."

"I should not impose," I said. "I'll be okay."

"Please," Shivaa said.

I agreed to stay.

"I am sorry but I cannot be much company," Kumar said. "I must be up early in the morning for work. This rain will bring in plenty of fish for me to gather. Please excuse me while I go to bed."

I gave him my contact information in case he wanted my help with the house while I was in Kolkata. I looked around the room and saw that there wasn't a phone anywhere, but perhaps he has access to one somewhere else. The man told the children that it was their bed time, and they gave me a hug, like I had been a part of the family for years, and went to bed. Everyone, but Shivaa and I, went to the other side of the curtain.

"What do you plan to do for the rest of the night?" I asked.

*You will feel. Me. Keep your eyes closed, and you will see
me.*

"I must get up early as well," she said. "Please make
yourself comfortable for the night."

From a stack of cloths kept on the floor, she pulled out
a blanket and a thin pillow.

Thunderous.

"Thank you," I said. "Well, goodnight."

"Goodnight," she said. "I probably will not see you in
the morning, but I will leave some food on the table for
breakfast. Please eat some."

"Thank you," I said.

Thank you for everything. This will be my last everything.

I noticed the anklet around her right ankle. It was red
and had tiny white beads jingling around it. She told me
goodnight again, and as she went to the other side of the
curtain, I realized that I didn't want the night to be over.
I lay on the mat and waited for the flashes of lightning to
appear through the window.

As my eyes drooped and as I turned to my side to sleep,
I heard a slight jingling. The sound became louder and
louder until it finally stopped. I felt a touch on my shoulder. I turned around and lay flat on my back. She bent
down and then she saddled me. She never said a word,
nor did I, as I was lost in a dreamlike state. She kissed
my lips. She kissed me repeatedly as she ran her hands
through my hair. My hands clenched her sides.

"Take me," she whispered. "I am already gone."

She stood up and walked away. The jingling of her anklet faded as quickly as it had increased a few minutes ago. I was left with the clash of electrical particles sounding outside.

I heard the birds chirp, and I felt the heat of the sunrise against my eyelids, but I continued to sleep. I heard a scream, but I still kept my eyes shut. After a second scream, I woke up. I stood up and looked around the house—empty. When I walked outside, I saw the children playing in the river, and I heard another scream. No one else was around. I walked around to the back of the house, where I saw Kumar—he was on his knees, facing a tree, with his hands raised to the sky. He wailed, and I ran to him to see if he was hurt.

Her body was dangling from one of the branches. I heard the jingling sound. She used the gossamer gown she wore last night as the noose—her body was bare except for the anklet she wore and it clinked as the wind blew. Kumar didn't look at me, but continued to cry—I knelt beside him and tried to comfort him, but his delirium kept me away.

She had her hair up like she didn't want it to get in the way of hanging herself. Her toenails and fingernails were painted red, and the small muscles in her stomach were showing. I saw that a piece of paper was nailed to the body of the tree. I ripped it off:

Now I can become a dream.

I knelt down on the roots of the tree and gazed at the

swaying body. She was a lifeless beauty. Her anklet jingled, and I began to cry.

Samosa

All he wore was a piece of blue cloth around his waist; he was bald and wore no shoes or sandals, and the shining whites of his eyes contrasted the dark color of his skin— like a soft boiled egg placed next to a burnt piece of bacon. He crouched and rested his back against the building of a clothing store. I stood outside of the building and watched Kolkata walk past me. Some carried briefcases, others held baskets on top of their heads—they all were going to work, I assumed. Some children dressed in blue sweater-vests and navy blue shorts biked to and from school with frowning faces, while other children, covered in torn brown and white cloths, played with the water pump, laughing and shouting, as their mothers went from car to car, person to person, asking for money or books. The buses sped as usual, the pedestrians screamed at the bus drivers as usual, the cars honked, the famished stray dogs searched through piles of trash and competed with the flies, and the homeless people lived without homes. It all made me wonder. It made me wonder, who are we? Who am I? We are all just animals.

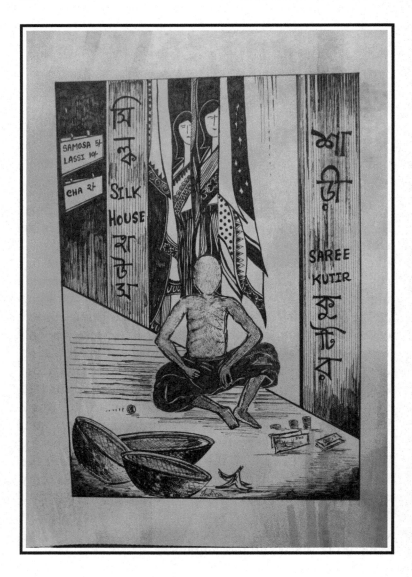

I assumed the man crouched against the clothing store was homeless. He took care of himself well though, as he squeezed lemon juice onto his hands to clean his fingernails. My knuckles stung as I ran my hands through my hair. I bit my knuckles, trying to create another pain. The man's skinny frame almost revealed the beating of his heart against his ribs. Mosquitoes hovered around his feet, but the insects didn't seem to bother him—they looked like they were worshiping the man, moving in a circular motion like some kind of ritual. He casually cleaned his fingernails and was oblivious to the rest of the world. I licked the tops of my hands.

I crouched down beside him to rest my legs, for I had been standing outside the building for twenty minutes observing everyone and everything. The winds caused by the fast-traveling vehicles helped bring the smell of fish, lentils, and lamb from the food huts down the street. I intended to stay for about another ten minutes before eating lunch—the smell of curry was quite appetizing. As I wiped my forehead, I heard a clinking sound and looked at the ground to see a few rupees rolling around. I guessed some pedestrians dropped it as they walked by. I didn't pick it up, but let them roll around for a few seconds until they lay still on the sidewalk. They stopped in between the homeless guy, who was still cleaning his fingernails, and me. He didn't pick the coins up, nor did he look at them. He continued to squeeze lemon juice onto his hands, and I rubbed my hands against my body. A few seconds later, another pedestrian dropped a couple of coins in front of us. I looked at the homeless man again, but he did not seem to notice the coins rolling on the ground. The rupees came to a stop between us. I looked at him and he threw the squished lemons to the edge of the sidewalk. The mosquitoes continued to hover around his feet.

"Take," a man said.

I looked up and saw a man dressed in brown slacks and a pink button-up collared shirt. He had neatly combed hair, which matched well with his finely trimmed mustache and beard. The man held some bills in his hand. He gently grabbed my arm and placed the bills in my hand, but I just let them drop to the ground.

"Take," he said. "Find some food."

He walked away.

"Sir," I said. "I do not want this money. I do not need any money. I am just resting my legs."

The man turned around, waved, and continued to walk away. He had given me five hundred rupees. I looked at the homeless man, and he was eating a banana. He took small bites and gently peeled it further after each taste. I felt dizzy—the world was going in circles around me, creating a whirring sound, a whirlpool in my head. The man did not look at me, nor did he look at the pile of bills I placed in the middle, where the coins were. After he finished the banana he threw it to the edge of the curb next to the lemons. He then proceeded to urinate against the wall of the clothing store. My stomach hurt. I gave him his privacy, looked the other way, and saw a woman drop some more coins in front of me.

"What are you doing?" I asked. "I am not homeless, nor am I a beggar. I don't need your money."

The lady smiled, touched my shoulder, and walked off.

"Take it," she said. "Find some food."

"I am not hungry."

She tilted her head and looked at me like I was a baby, distorting her face, scrunching it up, stretching her cheeks, and opening her mouth like she was about to drink from a straw. She placed her hand on my head and walked away.

The homeless man finished urinating and crouched back down. He began to sing and clap his hands. A group of people, after dropping a combination of coins and bills next to me, gathered around the lemon-scented man and began to clap in harmony with him. They stood in a circle and danced as the homeless man closed his eyes and beautifully sang a love song. I remained outside of the group but could not resist moving in rhythm to his voice as well. More coins were placed beside me. After the homeless man finished singing, the crowd dispersed, and he took out a mango and peeled it with a penknife. I was dehydrated; I tried to quench my thirst with my own saliva. Again, more pedestrians were giving me money, and I pushed it to the middle, but the homeless man did not appear interested in the accumulation of coins and bills.

"Take," one man said. "Find some food."

"No thank you," I replied. "I do not need any money. I have a home. I am not a beggar."

The man continued to walk away. The homeless man sucked on the seed of the mango. Not once did he look at me, nor at the money. I licked my lips.

"Hey," a man said. "Leave at once."

The man's voice was stern. I turned my head and saw a man who wore a security officer's uniform, dressed in all black. He had a thick mustache and parted hair. The top of his black boots came to his mid-shins, and his tan uniform was short sleeved and covered in dust. His belt was shiny. He must work for the clothing store, looking for thieves or any other kind of troublesome people.

"Leave at once," the man said.

I looked at the homeless man but he did not look at me or the security officer. He continued to suck on the mango seed.

"Me?" I asked.

The security officer pointed towards me and then to a direction down the street.

"Yes, you," he said. "Leave."

He stamped his foot against the sidewalk, trying to scare me. He clapped his hands, and then he raised them like he was going to slap me.

"Hut," he shouted. "Hut! Hut!"

"I'm just resting my legs," I said. "I am doing no harm."

"Go," the man said.

"Why?" I asked.

"You're getting in the way," he replied. "We don't let strays stay outside the store. It's bad for the business. The customers won't come anymore if they see beggars hanging around outside the store."

"I'm not a beggar," I replied. "It's shady here, and I just want to relax."

"Are you going to buy something?" he asked.

A man and a woman, holding hands, walked by and stopped and laughed.

"Go easy," the woman said. "It's hot. Give him some water."

"Then he will keep on coming back," the security officer said. "Move along."

The man placed some money at my feet, and the couple walked away.

"No," I said. "I don't need any thing."

"No loitering," the security officer said. "I will have you arrested."

"But this man here is homeless, and he's been sitting here just as long as I have," I said. "He is loitering as well then."

"I will have you arrested for loitering and troublemaking."

"But look at him," I said. "He's practically naked, and he urinated on your building, and he's been throwing lemons and banana peels. I am just sitting here."

I looked at the homeless man, who had finished sucking the juice from the mango seed, and he threw the seed and the mango peels to the edge of the curb where the lemons and the banana peel lay. He then proceeded to floss his teeth with a thin strip of the mango skin. My gums started to bleed—I spat and saw tiny dots of red in my spit.

"Take your money and go," the security officer said. "You have begged enough for the day. Find another place to bother."

"That's not my money," I said. "People have been dropping it here for some reason. I guess maybe for him."

I nodded my head towards the homeless man.

"Why aren't you telling him anything?" I asked.

"The store has strict policies." the guard replied. "We will lose customers because of you."

I stood up, and the homeless man remained crouched and silent. The security officer grabbed me by the ear and pulled me away from the front of the clothing store. He shoved me and I fell to the ground. The officer walked back into the building. I stood up, wiped the dust off my arms, and walked back to the front of the store. A young student, holding books in one hand, walked by and dropped some more coins next to my feet.

"Find some food," she said. "Take."

I kicked the coins against the building and cursed. My stomach hurt. I crouched down and splattered the wall with whatever was inside my intestines. The security officer came outside.

"Hey," the man shouted. "Come here. I will knock your head off. You swine."

The man started to run towards me. I spat on the window multiple times. When the security officer reached me, I gave him a slight push which caused him to stumble over. I picked up some of the money that was on the ground and ran away. A few blocks down, I found a small restaurant and waited by the trashcan. It was here, as I sniffed the contents of the bin, that I realized people had taken me for a mongrel.

"I am no mongrel," I shouted. "I am no mongrel!"

No one inside of the restaurant looked at me. Someone threw away a half-eaten samosa into the trashcan and exited the building.

This is My Head

My mother rang the doorbell to Tumar Uncle's run-down mansion; my father was also there. Only an hour before, I was arguing with both my parents, not wanting to go.

Visiting sick and old relatives was a bulk of our trips to Kolkata. Such occasions really took their toll on me. In the U.S., my life consisted of school, work, friends, music, and movies. That was basically it. I would go to college in the mornings, and then work at the clothing store at the mall, and after my shift, I would spend time with my friends listening to music or watching movies or hanging out at the café. When I would go to Kolkata, I was taken out of my world and placed in a reality that I was not accustomed to—a reality where death was near and sickness thrived. I knew cities in America also have many homeless and sick inhabitants, but it was nothing like it was in Kolkata. One of the memories I still have from a trip to my homeland was roughly 14 years ago, when I was seven years old—I walked out of the candy store, and I was immediately surrounded by beggars. These were not ordinary beggars though; these were kids the same age as

me, some younger. I had walked out of the shop, unwrap-
ping a Cadbury's chocolate bar with almonds, and as soon
as I was about to take my first bite, I felt arms tugging on
my shoulders. I was really small at the time, but I even
felt a few pulls on my knees—these were from the legless
one. The women were older, begging for some food, any
food, for their children. This one man, with no legs, had
a tuft of hair sprouting from the side of his head. The
few teeth in his mouth were black and yellow, crooked,
looking like the fence in our backyard after a hurricane.
His arms were nubs, ashy and red. I cannot remember his
eyes, for I couldn't look at them. I gave him a piece of
chocolate. I gave them all some chocolate, but once I had
given it all away, they continued to ask for more candy.
I wanted to go back inside with my parents to buy more
chocolate for them, but mother told me to keep walking.
That event was my first memory of reality.

The house took up a whole block of Theatre Road,
which was where most of my father's family lived. He
used to tell me stories about growing up on that street. Every Sunday, family and friends would gather at my grandmother's house, and they would sit in circles and hold
these singing sessions. I didn't know this grandmother too
well, because she died when I was a child, but she was a
very well known Indian singer. She would sing on the ra-
dio, perform concerts, and sell records. I asked my father,
once, what happened to the records, and he told me that
when she had died, one of the housekeepers must have
stolen them.

Someone opened the door four to five minutes later.
She wore a sari, which barely wrapped around her body,

and large circular glasses framed in brown plastic. Her hair was a mixture of grey and black, and it came down just below her shoulders. Her sandals revealed five bruised and worn toes on each foot.

Mother asked if we could visit with Tumar Uncle. She smiled and told us to come in. My last visit with Tumar Uncle, previous to this one, was three years ago. I remembered him as a happy man, always telling jokes and having fun with us. We followed her through the living room, or one of the living rooms, of the house. The innards of Tumar Uncle's mansion were covered in dust. It smelled of mothballs, and incense, and the black smoke coming through the windows, from the traffic, made my eyes water. I assumed that no one had come through his house for months, except for the housekeepers and cooks. From the living room, we walked upstairs and through several small hallways which gave us glimpses of some of the other rooms. Each step I took going up I wondered if it would all cave in. It was safer not to hold on to the railing. We continued to follow the lady and walked into a huge bedroom. It looked just as big as the living room. The bed didn't have any wrinkles, with its sheets neatly tucked under the mattress. I opened one of the armoires, and just before my mother told me to close it, in a stern voice, I saw a cockroach, as big as my ring finger, crawling on the inside wall. Strewn about on the dressers were pieces of jewelry—flashy earrings and necklaces laced with garnets and gold—and pictures. My mother pointed out to me a young Tumar Uncle in one of the photos. Another picture showed our relative's wife, who had passed away five years ago. My mother could not remember how she

died, but she wanted to say that she had set herself on fire
and burned to death. We walked through the bedroom
into a much smaller room which could easily have been
a walk-in closet. In it were only a small bed, a couple of
chairs, and a bed table. On the other side of the room was
a door leading out to the balcony. Tumar Uncle lay in the
bed on top of his bed sheets. I could immediately feel my
intestines unraveling as I look at this rusted man. I looked
at him in glances, trying hard not to stare. He still had
a head full of black hair and an unwrinkled brown face.
I could smell on his body the oils he used to keep himself fresh. He wore a white shirt, white pajama pants, and
black sunglasses. My father whispered in my ear that I
should go out onto the balcony while they talked to him
for a bit. They knew how I handled these kinds of situa-
tions. As I walked out, my mother asked Tumar Uncle to
remove his sunglasses from his face.

"Who's there?" Tumar Uncle said.

I walked past the bed, brushing against his snakeskin
feet. My mother told me to give *praṇām* before I went outside. I touched his feet and then my forehead and chest
to show my sign of respect for my elder, but Tumar Uncle
didn't say anything; he didn't give me his blessing. I sat
outside on the balcony of my uncle's mansion and looked
out onto the field where children played cricket and badminton. Kolkata summers were hot and without air con-
ditioners. I could feel the grime on the back of my neck
spread to my back. Though it was evening, the temperature would not drop till well into the night. I usually took
my bath late in the evening while the heat cooled and
transformed into the dark billows of Kolkatan pollution.

There were newly washed clothes hanging over clothes-lines that ran from one side of the balcony railing to the other. The smell of drying clothes was quite refreshing in contrast to the stench of the littered Kolkata streets— the smell of rotten banana peels and cow manure. The soap used to wash the clothes was nothing unusual, but I realized it smelt different when the clothes were hung outside compared to when taken out the dryer. The lazy breeze helped the scent to waver inside the balcony compartment. Near my feet was a bucket full of marigolds, which were used for praying rituals. There was also a broken armoire on the balcony, which I tried to open, but the doors would not budge. I could see and hear the inhabitants of the flats across from my uncle's house. One was cooking in the kitchen and shouting at a young girl for not washing her hands as she ate cookies. The woman wore a dark blue gown, and her teeth shone. Children played in the small field beneath me, as taxicabs and rickshaws bumped along the road, ignoring all pedestrians.

I thought about another relative, Ranga, who we had visited the last time we were in Kolkata three years ago. This was when I was about to start college, just before the new millennium. At the age of 99, he was the oldest man I'd ever met. He didn't look aged though. His skin was a healthy brown, oiled, and thick. He still had a bushy head of gray hair, which was neatly parted, and his eyebrows reminded me of those wild caterpillars shown on one of those television shows about nature. His beard went down to the ground, making him look like a fairy tale character in a children's book. When he would walk up the stairs, he would hold on to the railing with one hand, and with a walking cane in the other he would lean forward as much as possible; when he would walk down the stairs, he would lean back as much as possible. I always thought he would fall, but somehow, this was his homeostasis; this was the trick he had learned while coping with old age. My father and I were the only ones visiting him. We sat in his bedroom, and I listened to my father and this relative talk about other family members. I remember looking at his eyes—they were watery, like he had just woken up. As he spoke, he would scratch his head every now and then, and would gaze out the window, where the light entered through, warming our foreheads. I remember my father asking him what he thought about living through one full century. Ranga shook his head and said, "I wish not to see the next year." He said it in almost a whisper, like it was a secret. My father smiled and nodded his head. I didn't understand then why he wouldn't want to live for at least a full century, though later I realized that sometimes, one just does not want to live anymore. I didn't see him again after that visit, and now I wondered if his wish had come true.

My daze, lost in the scent of soap and marigolds, was interrupted by snarling. I looked towards the field and saw a dogfight; both dogs almost looked transparent, perhaps because their skins were tightly wrapped around their bones—they were street dogs. The children stopped their games of cricket and badminton and surrounded the battling mutts. They divided themselves into two sides. One group cheered for the brown dog while the other supported the black dog.

"Bite him," they yelled. "Bite him! Eat him!"

The dogs took turns in trying to grab hold of each other's neck, but both were quite quick and fierce. As they circled one another and snarled, the children continued to shout. I stood and leaned over the railing of the balcony to have a better view. The sun had gone down quicker than I expected, and the street lights had turned on. Again, the dogs went for each other's throat, and this time, the black dog was not quick enough. The children's rant became louder as the brown dog twisted and shook his enemy's body. After about ten seconds, the black dog stopped moving. The victor sniffed the body and then strolled off, and the children continued their games of cricket and badminton. Before the mosquitoes and ants could have their feast, I noticed a veiled woman, dressed in a sari, quickly run to the dead dog and drag it back into the shadows.

I felt a tap on my shoulder and jumped as I yelped. My father wanted me to go in and visit with Tumar Uncle before we all left. As I walked back into the room, I looked behind me, and saw that all the children were gone.

Tumar Uncle was speaking in Bengali with a raspy and quivering voice. My father told me that while I was outside, my mother had to repeatedly explain to him who we were, and she had to ask him again and again to take off his sunglasses. He didn't take them off until after I had walked back into the room. Tumar Uncle lifted his right hand, which was shaking, and removed his sunglasses. It shook until he placed the glasses on the bed. His eyes were bloodshot and he stared into the space in front of him. My mother and father sat on the bed beside him, and I sat on one of the chairs next to where he lay.

"It has been too long," Tumar Uncle said. He turned his head slowly, looked at my mother, and placed his left hand against her cheek for a few seconds. My mother then guided his hand to the bed and held it. Tumar Uncle again shifted his view from my mother's face to the space directly ahead of him. She spoke to him in a soothing voice, a voice that I had not heard since I was a crying child. She told him about our trip here, and she spoke of her father's health, which was becoming better. She commented on the humid weather and the crowded streets. Tumar Uncle did not respond. He did not move his head, speak, or do anything else. It was a silent illness. Nothing physically was wrong with him, but the problem seemed to be of the mental kind. My mother had mentioned earlier that he became a hermit once his wife died, and she had heard that he'd left his house only a few times in the five years since. He did not talk to anyone. He barely moved about, and he rarely spoke. On the way to his room, the housekeeper had said that he had a huge bedroom, but chose to live in the smallest room of the house.

Tumar Uncle gazed into the space directly in front of him. I glanced at the wall opposite where he lay and noticed a picture on the wall. The picture was full of colors and had a figure in the foreground. I knew it was one of the Hindu gods, but I was not sure which one. I asked my father, and he told me that the goddess was Kali, who was the goddess of destruction, and the source of the Kolkata's name.

"Baba," I said, "what happened to Ranga?"

"Actually," my father said. "I don't quite know. But did you know that he was your Buli Mashi's brother?"

"Yes," Tumar Uncle said. "Ranga-da. He is gone. He is dead."

"When did he pass?" I asked.

I cleared my throat. Tumar Uncle still hadn't looked at me yet, and I wondered if he knew if I was even there, or if he was talking to a voice in his head.

"Before this new year," he said. "Cremated. I want to burn too."

I looked at my father, who was staring at the cracked marble floor.

Without turning his head, Tumar Uncle pointed to me and asked who I was. My father placed his hand on my shoulder and told him that I was their son.

"You last saw him three years ago," my mother said. "He is our son."

Tumar Uncle did not respond and continued to point at me. I wanted to say hello, but I was nervous and felt out of place, so I started to pace back and forth in the small space between his bed and the wall.

"His name is Rajesh," my mother said. "You used to hold him in your arms and play games with him. I remember how you would carry him on your shoulders."

I had no recollection of being around him when I was a child, but from what my mother said, Tumar Uncle and I had spent a lot of time together. He would put me on his shoulders and walk around the house, pretending that we were on some kind of adventure, or he would make up games for us to play. The housekeeper entered the room and asked us if we wanted any drinks or some sweets. My parents and I politely declined and Tumar Uncle remained motionless and speechless.

"Tumar-da," the housekeeper said, "would you like some lemon tea and biscuits?"

Tumar Uncle stared at the picture of Kali, then rubbed

his hand across his face as one does to see if a shave was needed. He then slapped himself.

"She is not my wife," Tumar Uncle said. "She is not Buli."

"No," mother said. "She is not Buli Mashi."

The housekeeper walked away mumbling to herself.

"Where is Buli," Tumar Uncle asked.

He began to speak in English rather than in Bengali.

"Buli Mashi is not here," mother said. "She has passed on."

"Dead," Tumar Uncle said.

He repeated the word, but he said it in Bengali. I was ready to leave. We had only been there for about ten minutes, but the small room seemed to have elongated time. I was used to seeing my other ill-stricken relatives, but they were mostly physically sick. They were still cheerful, joked, drank tea, and laughed. Tumar Uncle was different. He lay on the bed, but at the same time, he was not there. His mind had dissolved into the humid air of his mansion, and all that remained was his body and the picture of Kali on the wall. I tried to visualize him as the man in the photograph that stood on the dresser in the bedroom next door, but I could not come up with anything. I could not imagine him as a young and happy man, for all I saw was this decrepit man who lay in bed next to me. I wondered if he could dream anymore. I could only think that the recollections he still had were of his wife. I looked around the room to ease my discomfort, noticing the cracks on the floor, the walls, and the ceiling. In the far corner of the room, placed on a wooden chair with three legs, was a suit, creased and dusty.

"Sit here," Tumar Uncle said.

I looked at my parents, and they moved aside so I could sit next to him on the bed. I slowly walked towards him, but I remained standing. Tumar Uncle grabbed and tugged my arm until I had no choice but to sit. His hand was cold and rough. I couldn't see any calluses on his palm, but it felt like it was covered with them. I looked at the skin of his arm and noticed its thinness and papery texture. It was almost transparent, and I imagined staring straight through his skin, observing a thick medium of black blood trickling towards his heart. His breath smelled of cloves and tea, and I had to look away just to breathe. As I sat closer to him, I saw some sadness in his haunting red eyes—a whirlpool of decay within his pupils. I imagined entering these crumbling tunnels to see what was inside, and all I could envision was fiery intestines, lungs, and kidneys. A hell within his body.

"I am dead," Tumar Uncle said.

"You are still alive," I managed to say. "We are all here. We are all living."

My voice quivered. His voice was scratchy and firm.

"Shouldn't we be going?" I asked my parents.

"I am crazy," Tumar Uncle said. "Watch me corrode."

"We are all crazy," I replied.

"I was once happy," he said. "But now, I have nothing. Buli is gone."

"Yes," I said. "Buli Mashi is gone."

"Dead," Tumar Uncle said. "I am just a cockroach."

"We are all cockroaches."

"No. I am a cockroach. Life won't let me die. Look in the cupboards, the closets, I am there, praying to be taken."

I remained silent until he spoke again. He grabbed my arm again and placed it on top of his head. It was oily. If I had put just enough pressure, I felt like I could break through his skull.

"This is my head," Tumar Uncle said.

I took his arm and placed it on top of my head.

"This is my head," I said.

Tumar Uncle laughed and held my hand. It sounded like a mixture of laughing, hyperventilating, crying, and coughing. His eyes were wide open and he shook up and down as he lay on the bed. His laugh became louder and he began to shriek as if he was being murdered. He moved his head back and forth and flapped his arms up and down. I stood, but I didn't move away from the bed. My parents took a step back and motioned me to get away, but I did not walk away. I couldn't walk away; I was frozen. His hand was now clasped around mine. This was what I could only imagine death felt like. I thought about Ranga gazing out the window, into the sun, resembling a holy statue of some sort.

"Please," I said. "Please, let go."

I peeled his fingers off and placed his hand next to his body. Tumar Uncle clutched my arm again and pulled me close to his mouth, forcing me to sit down again. Spit came out as he continued to cackle and cry. I pictured Ranga leaning forward as he walked up the stairs, like he was looking for a fallen contact lens on each step. I looked at Tumar Uncle's face, and he was crying. His red eyes were producing tears that fell slowly, almost lazily.

"Why won't they let me die," Tumar Uncle shouted. "I

want to go."

I squinted my eyes and turned my face to the side so the spit did not enter my eyes. A small amount of drool surrounded his mouth. He moved my arm up and down and started to slap his own face with his other arm. I placed my free hand against his cheek to cushion any damage done to his face. The smacks stung my hand, and it began to throb immediately, reminding me how my father used to tell me that when he was in school in England, the teacher would slap their wrists with rulers whenever they were in trouble. Both my parents tried to grab me, but I motioned to them to stay away. My right leg shook, causing the bed to creak.

Tumar Uncle stopped hitting himself, and my hand, but he continued to shake and cry.

"This is what I have become," he said. "A dying baby. Lonesome and crazy."

I put my hand against his forehead and felt the sweat and rising temperature of his body. He stopped all his motions, and he stopped making any kind of sounds; he stared into the space before him as he was doing when we first entered the room.

"Sleep," my mother said. "Go to sleep and get some rest."

My mother left the room to get the housekeeper. My father stayed with me and we stood in silence. The quietness was the kind that seeped into my skin and made me want to scream or jump. A few minutes later, my mother came back with the housekeeper. We said goodbye to Tumar Uncle, but he didn't respond. The housekeeper held a dampened handkerchief in her hand and a glass of water.

Both my parents walked out, and I followed.

I turned around and looked at him one last time before I left, because I did not think I would ever see him again. He had already put his sunglasses back on his face. As I walked through the door, I heard him speak.

"This is my head," Tumar Uncle said.

Backward

Kama flew backward and hit his back against the wall—there was no one else around him. He rubbed the rear of his head and looked left and right. He felt like he needed to speak. He felt like he should say something to justify his actions.

He spoke: "I am compelled to."

Four seconds later the barista came out from the back of the *café*, tying an apron around her waist. She had black hair and a tattoo of a solid black line going around her neck. She noticed Kama's position—sitting on the floor, against one of the walls of the coffee shop. She saw that his drink had been knocked down and that the chair had fallen over. Kama stood up and retied his shoelaces. He looked at her like he had just seen her for the first time. He always looked at her that way—covering her body with his eyes, observing her auburn skin and the wide curvature of her breasts, her brown eyes and pointed nose. Every time he looked at her, he saw nothing but a tiny ball of colorful energy—splashes of blues and reds and greens and oranges. She blew him away.

"Damn time," he said. "Kali, can I get another *chai*?"

Kali picked up the chair and straightened the table.

"What happened now?" she asked.

"I flew back and hit the wall," Kama said.

"Again? Stop it."

"Sorry."

"This is the last one."

She went behind the counter and made Kama a *chai* for the third time. For each drink, he was getting further and further away. As he walked toward her to pay for the drink, he flew backward until he hit the front of the *café*, rattling the glass door.

"Sheesh," Kama said.

"Stop," Kali said. "It's not going to happen."

"Give me one more chance. It'll work this time. I can feel it."

"We're just friends," she said.

Kama stood up and flew back again, through the door and onto the sidewalk. He crawled back inside and grabbed one of the legs of the nearest table.

"Move on," Kali said. "I adore you. I really do. But move on."

"I love you."

"Yes you do."

Kama's legs lifted; with his hand grasping the leg of the table, he hovered and clenched his teeth. He held on with one hand and stuck the other in his pocket, pulling out a bracelet.

"We can't keep going back to this," Kali said. "Let's just keep going on. You got your way, and I got my way."

"One last go," Kama said.

He managed a smile and tossed the bracelet to Kali and let go of the table at the same time. He flew backward, through the door, over the sidewalk, over the road, over the traffic lights, over the buildings—he kept going the other way. He went and went and went until he forgot about time. Kali wrapped the bracelet around her wrist and looked through the glass door. She looked to where time didn't exist.

Tagore's Kiss

The echoes in Kolkata's Victoria Hall Coffee House were vibrant and gloomy. As I sat at a table and read Tagore's "The Living and the Dead," the indiscreet murmur of the room settled into my head rather than Tagore's words. I folded the top corner of the leaf and closed the book. I looked around the *café*, which seemed more like a great banquet hall, and observed the other people. They laughed, talked, coolly smoked cigarettes, and sipped coffee. The baristas wore black collared shirts with white aprons and stumbled their way through the aisles to appease their customers. Some consumers studied their textbooks, while others pretended to study and glanced around the room trying to make eye contact with the opposite sex. The second level of the *café* was full as well. People leaned over the railing and looked down at us on the first floor just as we peered up at them. Nothing too scenic, but I realized that whenever there was a second floor to any building, I always wanted to be up there, especially if there was a railing so I could look over at the people downstairs. I took my book and cup of tea and found a table on the second floor.

The second level of Victoria Hall Coffee House was more of a leisure section than the first. No studying took place there, only conversation. I was the only one with a book on the second floor. A couple of people looked at me as I held my book, probably trying to let me know that if I wanted to read, I should go back downstairs. Despite their scowls, I took a sip and ordered a refill of my tea.

As I looked around, I noticed there were a lot more conversations between men and women on the second level than on the first floor. There seemed to be more flirting and smiling at one another up here. People laughed louder, talked louder, clapped their hands with great emphasis, and smoked their cigarettes like they owned Victoria Hall Coffee House. I suspected that no one older than the age of twenty-five was on the second floor, including myself.

I noticed that despite the flirting and sexual tension between the males and females, there was no touching, hugging, or kissing. In America, especially in the *cafés*, there were always people holding each other's hand, or someone's arm placed over another person's shoulder. There was always some kind of physical contact between people to show some affection. In Kolkata, I had never seen this physical display of amity. I had visited many friends and family, and I had rarely seen, if at all, a kind of touch between a husband and wife. I also had never—to my knowledge—met anyone who was in a relationship without being married. It was either one was married, or one was alone. What I saw on the second floor of Victoria Hall Coffee House, I thought was cute. There was this strong energy of love, affection, or tension, but none shown through the touch of fingertips, just in the glances of the eye, or a perfectly formed smile.

"Your tea sir," the waitress said.

She placed the saucer and cup on my table with a couple of packets of sugar and a small flask of cream. She was gorgeous—shoulder length black hair, smooth brown eyes, no cosmetics, and coffee-cream colored skin. She wore a black skirt that ended a few inches above the top of her ankle. Even the way she wore her black-laced scuffled shoes was exquisite. She had the sleeves of her button-up white shirt rolled up, which revealed the red and orange bangles that clanged around her thin wrists. They matched the bracelets that danced around her right ankle.

"Thank you," I said.

She nodded and looked at my Tagore book before walking away. I stirred the cream into my tea and continued to look around the room. The aura of the room, as it vibrated against the walls of Victoria Hall Coffee House put me in a daze. About half an hour later, the waitress came back.

"More tea?" she asked.

"Yes, please."

She looked at my book again.

"Are you from here?"

"I'm from America, but my family is from here," I said. "I'm visiting my grandparents, and then I go back to college in a couple of weeks."

She finished pouring the tea, and it looked like she wanted to say something, but just as she was about to open her mouth, she walked away.

"Thank you," I said.

She probably didn't hear me. However, only moments later, she came back.

"What are your thoughts on Tagore?" she asked.

Her question caught me off guard, and I sipped the tea to give myself time to think. When I looked up at her, I was caught off guard again by the way she looked. So pretty.

"I'm reading now, 'The Living and the Dead,'" I said.

As I was about to continue, she spoke.

"Yes. 'Jībita o Mṛta.' Such a tragedy," she said. "Such suffocation."

Before I could reply, she walked away again. I sat there, losing track of time. I sipped tea, smoked tasteless cigarettes, and listened to the murmur that surrounded me. I still didn't notice a touching of anyone's skin, a hug, or a holding of hands. People wanted to, I knew they all wanted to, but something kept them back—maybe it was tradition and custom, or a show of respect, or a revealing of the shy side of Indian culture.

Whatever it was, although I was an Indian, I could not abide by it.

Every so often, the waitress would come and bring me more tea. I pretended that I wanted more each time she visited though, really, I just wanted to be around her. I was done with the tea, tired of it. I couldn't concentrate on reading anymore, as my thoughts traveled toward the waitress. Each time she came, we would talk about Tagore's story, and love and tragedy. I had been there, now, for at least two and a half hours.

Again, the waitress came back, brushing my shoulder.

"Your refill, sir," the waitress said.

I felt somewhat awkward when she called me "sir," for I suspected we were about the same age.

"Thank you," I replied.

Before she walked away, she looked at my book again.

"I also enjoy his poetry very much. *Gītāñjali* is marvelous."

"I love *Gītāñjali*," I said. "I first started off by reading his poetry and then moved on to his stories. I think I will read *A Grain of Sand* next."

"It is quite the novel, sir. I hope you will enjoy it. It's amazing what we will do for love—the willingness to go beyond what is expected of us, to go where love takes us, whether it's right or wrong."

"Tagore is a master at showing the beauty of the disaster which love can create," I said.

I felt bad. I was probably trying to come off as some kind of Tagore expert, when I was just an ordinary reader. She, who most likely grew up in Kolkata, must have known more about the writer than I. She'd have read his works in Bengali, not in some English translation.

"He is also a beautiful song writer as well," I said.

She closed her eyes and sang.

"A vein of lightning, a beautiful, sudden sight, an image lost and found, you charge the storm with a reeling presence."

Her voice was beautiful, and though she sang in a quiet voice, the world around me was muted, and it was just us.

"The sky deepens, the river wedges, waves in a vehement quest, with nameless desires, dreams, unrealized."

She opened her eyes and looked at me, as she finished the song.

"Tears of suffering and pain, hollering, hovering in each horizon."

I was speechless. I didn't know what to say. I just kept looking into her eyes, as the words simmered inside of me.

"That is one of my favorite Tagore songs," she said. "It's an English translation of 'Dekhā Nā Dekhāy.'"

I realized that if I didn't say anything soon, she would walk away, and I didn't want her to walk away. I wanted her to sit and chat about Tagore and the weather. I wanted her to sing to me some more. I looked around the room and became dizzy—I had not eaten anything all day. I stood up and stumbled. She grabbed my arm. She looked at me and licked her lips.

"Okay?" she asked.

"Thank you for the tea," I said.

Then, without thinking, I kissed her. In front of everyone, on the second level of Victoria Hall Coffee House, I kissed her, and she kissed me back. She placed her hands around my body, and my hands touched the back of her head. All the murmur and all the echoes deafened for a few seconds as our lips touched. As I took a step back, I noticed her flushed face. I was smiling, but she was not. She knew she was in trouble. We stood there and looked at each other for a few seconds without saying anything. Then, as I looked around the room, I noticed a small crowd had formed around us. There was a lot of yelling and whistling. I was sure she was embarrassed, though I felt nothing but joy.

"Shara! Shara!" a man shouted.

A man pushed his way through the crowd. He wore the Victoria Hall Coffee House colors, as well as a nametag which read, "Manager." He was an older man, probably around his sixties. His head full of gray hair was slicked back. A thin-framed set of glasses rested on his nose, and I could smell his cologne, which seemed a mixture of fruit and formaldehyde.

"Shara!" he said. "What are you doing? What do you think this is? This is not a place to be kissing your customers. I am not the manager of some bordello. Shara! Listen to me!"

I looked at Shara, who stared at the floor. The manager began to speak in Bengali, of which I could only understand a little. He continued to shout at her—and I realized that her name meant "move" or "get out." My mother would say "Shara" to me when I was much younger and constantly getting in her way as I played.

"It was my fault," I said. "She had nothing to do with it."

The manager either did not hear me, or chose not to listen to what I said. He continued to yell. Shara began to cry. She never looked at me again but only stared at the marble floors of Victoria Hall Coffee House. As the manager shouted, everyone else around us listened or gave their input on the situation. The manager finally took her by her upper arm and roughly guided her to the back where only the employees could go.

I was left with the crowd. They spoke in Bengali, and I couldn't really make out what they were saying, but by the looks on their faces, I didn't think it was anything too nice. I paid my check, placed the money on the table, and left my fresh cup of tea to waste. As I walked down the stairs, I could feel eyes staring at the back of my neck. People who were downstairs were standing as well, looking at me. One man asked me what had happened. I didn't respond, but exited Victoria Hall Coffee House. A couple of blocks down, I realized that I had left my Tagore book on the table, but I didn't bother to go back and get it. I was thinking about the kiss that echoed against the walls of Victoria Hall Coffee House.

Bullies

There were six of them—none taller than five feet or shorter than four. They were a pack of black eyes and bloody lips and spiky hair. Every time Rajesh drove by them he looked the other way—he never wanted trouble. He just wanted to go home, eat dinner, and watch TV until he fell asleep. The next day—go to work, and then do the same thing. He had been successful for a long time—he hadn't crossed their paths for a year. Sometimes Rajesh took detours, and other times, he was able to park in his driveway without any worry because they were fishing at the river just outside of the neighborhood.

He had been lucky up until five weeks ago when, as he pulled into the driveway and stepped out of the car, he had found himself surrounded by the bullies. They had been waiting on the side of the house he couldn't see—a blind spot. He usually made sure to drive past the house to check the other side, and then back up and pull into the driveway. Rajesh wasn't thinking clearly that day as it had been a long day at the office.

They threw steaming lentils at his car, and then at him. They hit his knees, and his face, and his stomach—

it burned. The mush was in his hair and eyes, and when some hit his nose, he fell to the ground, screaming and jerking around trying to wipe off the lentils. Every now and then, between the pelts, Rajesh saw his car covered in the vegetable, bits and pieces sliding down the driver-side windows.

As he was on the ground, they went up to him and pointed and laughed. Some kicked his feet, while others made sure the mashed potatoes had covered any clean spots of skin. There were a few seconds of silence, and then Rajesh felt a warm liquid being poured onto all of his body. Some went into his mouth—chutney. He had to make sure that he didn't choke on it.

Grabbing onto his legs and arms, the kids dragged Rajesh into the front yard and rolled him around in the grass. He tried to stand up, but the bullies had too much of an advantage and were able to keep him down. He wasn't sure how long the torture had lasted, but at one point, when he opened his eyes, there was no one around. Rajesh went inside his house and cried in the bathroom before calling the police.

Rajesh showed the policeman his wounds—his cuts and bruises, and some spots of burned skin. He showed him his car and the lentils on the driveway. The officer asked Rajesh if he could describe the gang—he told him that they were short and skinny and that they all had spiky hair and they wore colorful T-shirts and shorts. He said that they were probably not older than ten to thirteen, and the police officer laughed. Rajesh said it wasn't funny. He said he wanted some kind of protection. The police officer wrote it all down and said he would ask around and investigate.

Rajesh never heard back from him, and the neighborhood was quiet for two weeks. Sometimes, he would see his neighbors coming and going from their houses, but none of them ever looked at him. They knew not to. They knew they could be next.

Last week, Rajesh saw the bullies riding around on their bikes—a couple with training wheels, while others had moved on up to the standard bicycles. They stared at him as he passed them by. They were smiling, and they all started shouting, "lentils," and pointing at him. Rajesh sped up and made the corner, screeching and swerving, almost driving into his living room. As he ran into his house from the car, leaving the driver-side door open, he saw the kids making the turn around the corner. All of the doors were locked—the front door, the side door, the back door. Rajesh was safe. They could have done whatever they wanted to his car—drenched it in lamb curry or soup. He didn't care as long as they weren't able to drag him into the front yard.

The morning after, Rajesh found a note on his windshield, reading, "Dinner will be served."

During the following week, Rajesh acquired a pistol— he kept it in the glove compartment. He took shooting lessons. He didn't want to live in fear anymore— the bullies had taken over his psyche. At the office, the boss had taken his son in to see what his job consisted of, and Rajesh hid under his desk for two hours, until the boss's son left. Rajesh stopped going to the park, too—he just couldn't be around children without thinking of steaming lentils. He was going to sign up for PTSD counseling, but he wanted to find a quicker way to ease his mind—he thought that getting a firearm was the easiest solution.

Yesterday evening, when Rajesh pulled into the driveway, he saw the six bullies standing in the front yard and their bicycles leaning on their kickstands on the sidewalk. The bullies stood with the arms folded, except for one—the leader, who was shorter than everyone else but stockier. He wore a tank-top, and he was stirring a large pot full of steamed vegetables—carrots, broccoli, cauliflower, lettuce, corn. Rajesh could smell the dish as he rolled up his window. He took his pistol out of the glove compartment and put it in his pocket before stepping out. He didn't look at them—he didn't say anything to them, and he tried to walk towards the front door. The bullies stepped in front of him, not saying anything. The bullies' heads barely reached Rajesh's shoulder. He tried to move around them, but one of the bullies tripped him, causing Rajesh to stumble into the bullies' bicycles. The leader picked up the pot of vegetables and poured it over him. As Rajesh stood up, he pulled out his pistol, but the bullies were just as quick, and each kid pulled out his own gun and aimed it at Rajesh. He tilted his head to the side and looked at their firearms, and just as he was about to pull the trigger, the bullies shot their guns in unison. Two seconds later, Rajesh lay face down in the front yard with spots of red forming on the back of his neatly tucked in button-up shirt. The leader picked up the large pot and they all got back on their bicycles and rode away.

When the police arrived ten minutes later, Rajesh's house was surrounded by his neighbors. The officers asked them what they had seen, but they all looked down, or away, or said that they hadn't seen or heard anything. The front yard smelled of steamed vegetables, but the police couldn't find any leads. They went back the following morning, including the officer who had been there for the lentils incident. The officer looked around and saw a group of kids riding their bikes—they waved to him, and he nodded his head and waved back, telling them to be careful and to watch out for cars. The bullies kept riding their bikes until they reached the river, and they pulled out their fishing poles and looked for turtles and frogs.

A Good Conversation

Every Sunday, when I would walk home from the market I would see a man sitting on the porch of a house on the road. He wore a straw hat, with ripped slacks, black shoes, and a blue kurta. His eyes were always red—they glared at me every week. One time, as I held a bag of lettuce and tomatoes, he called to me with a grunt. I waved and continued to walk but he grunted again and motioned me to come visit.

I stood at the foot of his porch; he looked at me for a few seconds before he said that I look like I needed a good beating. I asked him why. Because he didn't like me, he said. I asked him again why. Because he didn't like my eyes.

I looked at his, red and narrow. I didn't know what else to say, so I walked off to the sound of him cackling and coughing. That happened every week for about a month. The last time was about a month ago, and I haven't seen him on the porch since. I've wondered where he went, and I've missed those red vicious eyes.

Maybe I did need a good beating. He did scare me a bit, but nonetheless, he was the only person I talked to on Sundays.

Kenneth's Enlightenment and the Reincarnation of Cub

Kenneth stood at the edge of the cliff, an ocean of stone below him, and as he looked up, he saw the sky, blue and quiet and cloudless. A hawk floated. It dropped and rose, dropped and rose, like it was trying to stay awake. Kenneth turned his head and saw Cub; he was plump for his height—belly sticking out, hanging over his waist, and he had just reached the 4 foot mark. He would be Hardy. Kenneth would be Laurel—skinny legs, skinny body, skinny nose. He turned his head back around.

"This is pretty," Kenneth said, not looking back. "I mean, this is beautiful. India, India."

Cub rubbed his belly.

"Enjoy this," Kenneth said. "The sky. Look at it. So big. So quiet. Away from everything. All the cameras. All the people. All the work. So fake. This is real. Do you see that bird? What's that bird feeling?"

Kenneth took off his shirt. He started unbuckling his

belt. Soon he was naked—he wore only his shoes, covered in plastic grocery bags. He closed his eyes.

"The world is a tub," he said.

He opened his eyes and looked behind him—but Cub wasn't there. Kenneth turned in a circle, but Cub was nowhere around. He looked for his clothes, but they were gone as well. Kenneth felt cold.

"This isn't funny, Cub," Kenneth said. "Give me my clothes back."

Kenneth shouted Cub's name repeatedly. The words echoed. The sky was hollow. The hawk was no longer there. Kenneth walked back to the trail.

"Get back to the cabin," he told himself.

He started to jog. He ran.

The plastic bags covering his shoes tore off.

He stared at them—bright and white. He licked his finger and wiped off a smudge of dirt at the heel of one his shoes.

"Cub," he whispered. "Where are you?"

It was dark. Kenneth couldn't find the path to the cabin. He sat down, crossed legged under a banyan tree growing out of a large rock. He closed his eyes and rested his head against the body of the tree.

"Dad is going to be mad."

Kenneth slept for three days. He awoke covered in dirt and twigs and moss—he didn't wipe them off. Ants crawled around his kneecaps, and his remaining shoe was no longer bright and white. He saw pathways through the woods—rows of halls that had been hidden to him.

He started running again and found himself at another cliff. There was a large tent, and not too far away from it, a small firepit. Kenneth shouted hello. The tent shook, and the door was unzipped.

A head popped out: "Wow. You're naked. Look Anita."

A black haired head popped out above the guy's. Her mouth opened and she pushed the guy out of the tent and rushed to Kenneth, almost stumbling into him.

"I'm a huge fan," she said. "Can I have your autograph? Jaya, get some paper. Anything. A leaf."

Jaya pulled his backpack out from the tent and started looking through it, pulling out a pen and a notepad. He handed them to Kenneth.

"How come you're naked?" Anita asked.

He signed his autograph on the notepad and handed it to Anita. She went inside the tent and came out with a white skirt and a black spaghetti strap shirt.

"Sorry," she said. "But this is all I have. Jaya?"

"The only clothes I got are the ones I'm wearing right now."

Kenneth looked at the clothes in Anita's hands.

"I'll trade you my shoe for them."

He started to take his shoe off, but Anita insisted that he keep it. He put on the skirt and shirt.

"Are you shooting an episode here in India? Bombay?" Jaya asked. "Where's Cub?"

"Where's Cub?" Kenneth repeated.

Jaya and Anita shrugged their shoulders.

"You haven't seen him by any chance?" Kenneth asked. "Can't seem to find him anywhere."

"This is just like the episode when you couldn't find him while you all were at the mall," Anita said.

"So tell me," Jaya said. "What does it feel like to be so

famous at such a young age? You have a huge following over here."

Kenneth looked into the sky and saw a hawk soaring in the air.

"He was here one second, and gone the next," he said.

Kenneth fiddled with his skirt and kicked a fallen branch.

"Cub was always there for me," he said. "He always took care of me, especially now, as it's easy to get lost in the entertainment world.

He traced his fingers through the dirt.

"I need him to take care of me."

There was a loud growling, and a 10 foot black bear appeared from the woods, standing on its hind legs. Jaya and Anita retreated into the tent. They whispered to Kenneth, telling him to get inside, but he remained outside.

"Cub," Kenneth said.

The bear walked up to Kenneth and sniffed him. Kenneth sniffed back.

"We are special," Kenneth said.

The bear swung at Kenneth—its paw barely missing Kenneth's cheek. He maneuvered around the black bear and punched it in the back of the head. As it turned around, Kenneth kicked the stomach. A baby bear flew out of its mouth.

"Cub."

The black bear sniffed around and then looked at Kenneth.

"He's mine," Kenneth said.

The black bear wandered off.

Kenneth crouched down, and the baby bear climbed onto his back—holding a white shirt in its mouth.

"What happened, Cub?"

"Rrrrrrr," the baby bear said.

The cub licked Kenneth's face. Anita and Jaya came out of the tent. Kenneth kissed Cub on the forehead.

"I got to take him back to the cabin," Kenneth said. "We should get back to the U.S. Our parents are going to be mad."

"But it's a cub," Anita said.

"It's Cub," Kenneth said. "Look at his paws."

Jaya and Anita looked at each other, and then at Kenneth. Kenneth couldn't see their faces. Kenneth couldn't see anything. Everything was covered in the sun's light.

"What's going to happen to the show?" Anita asked.

Kenneth looked at the cub.

"Looks like the writers have some work to do," he said. "Show me the way back, Cub."

He thanked Jaya and Anita for their kindness. The baby bear pulled on Kenneth's skirt and led the way.

"Come on, Cub," Kenneth said. "We got to go home."

Above, in the sky, a hawk flew in circles, making some kind of halo over the world.

"Rrrrrrr," the baby bear said.

"Some vacation," Kenneth said. "Can't see anything but light, but we'll make it back home."

The cub sighed.

"I'll take care of you," Kenneth said.

Empty Chair

"Imran has been shot," I said. "He's by the generator. But I was able to take two of them down by the bushes. We got to make sure to go back and find Imran's body. He deserves a proper burial."

"Right," Kahn whispered. "I know there are some enemies by those lamp posts. They have situated themselves in that ditch."

"That'll be tough," I reply. "Too much open area. We should get them from behind. I'm almost out of bullets."

"I've plenty," Kahn said. "Where are Walid and Salman?"

"They are staged in the right flank, north of where we are. They were able to scramble to that small bunch of bushes ahead of us. In our last contact, they were heading for the main house, where Joe is hiding. Once we capture him, we've won. We control the whole area."

"Come on," Kahn said. "Let's make our way around to surprise them in the ditch. We'll make it our own stronghold."

We headed south, down a side road, and crawled through the fields. We were sure we'd be ambushed in the grass, but no one was there. If we could take away their station at the ditch, and the others could get Joe, we would be in excellent position. Our allies were securing the surrounding areas, and we would gain control of Parkway View. We'd lost a lot of men, but we all kept thinking that it was for a good cause—to control our own freedom, and to control the freedom of others. The war had been going on for about a week, which was longer than we expected. The enemies were not surrendering, but using all their might to defend themselves. I wanted it to all be over. I wanted to be home with my family, eating dinner and watching television. The heat was unbearable, thick with humidity, and with an enemy. I wanted to end it all before night came, for I didn't think I could fight through another fiery day. I could tell Kahn was ready to go home as well. He missed his sister. He missed his bed. As we made our way to the ditch, I kept thinking of Imran and how he had had his whole future taken away. I pictured him covered in red and rolling around to stop the agony of those bullets immersed in his stomach. We had all envisioned a quiet war with minimal casualties, but now we found ourselves in the fight not only for our lives, but for the lives of others—our families and friends, our neighbors, and our world. It all came down to us, and I was ready to release the burden that lay on the shoulders of our soldiers.

My dreams of future harmony died as I felt the beads spilling red all across my back. The pain caused me to fall and scream. We had been attacked from the back. I could see Kahn, who tried his best to fight back, but soon he lay on the ground beside me. That was it. We had failed.

I thought of Imran, and how he must have gone through the same feelings. The enemies were already gone. They'd shot us and left to shoot more. I looked into Kahn's eyes as we faced each other laying in the dirt. His eyes were tearing as he took his last breaths.

"Sorry," I whispered.

"Sorry," Kahn replied.

He closed his eyes and let the bloodstained dirt become his new home. I tried to keep my eyes opened as long as possible. I breathed every breath to its fullest, hoping for the possibility of being saved. In distant echoes I could hear my mother call me, as she would always call me:

"Roy," she shouted. "Come in. It's time for dinner. Wash up and set the table. Roy. Roy. Hurry in."

I could hear her voice sounding stronger and stronger. She was calling my name as I was dying next to my dead friend. I closed my eyes and pictured my family.

"Roy," mother shouted. "Hurry in. Call your friends. Dinner is ready."

I opened my eyes and rolled on my back. I wiped the dirt off my pants and checked my elbows for scrapes. No serious damage was done. I looked at Kahn, who continued to lay with his eyes closed.

"Kahn," I said. "Come on. It's time for dinner. Mother is calling us."

Kahn opened his eyes and looked around. He rubbed the dirt off his pants, and stood up.

"Already," he said. "Well, I'm hungry anyway."

We walked towards my house where Imran was waiting for us.

"Hurry," Imran said. "I'm starving."

"That was fun," I said.

I turned around and saw Joe, Walid, and Salman walking towards my parents' house. We were all going to eat dinner together, and they were also spending that night at my house for my birthday celebration. There would be one empty chair at the crowded table, though, left there to remind us of my older brother. He is no longer around. He is gone. He has been gone for four years, and he will never come back.

"What should we do after we eat?" Salman asked.

"Let's watch a movie," Joe replied.

We all agreed to Joe's suggestion and went inside the house to get ready for dinner. We planned to watch *Masters of the Universe*. My brother and I would watch it all the time—to where we knew all the words. After every time we saw it, we would go outside and act out the movie. We won't be able to watch it together anymore.

A Grave Clown

Abhra sat on his bed with his elbows resting on his knees. His face hid in his hands as his feet rubbed against the gray carpet. As the phone rang, he looked at the alarm clock and realized that he had been sitting on his bed for a half hour.

He washed his face and stared at himself in the mirror, seeing the red in his eyes.

"I have to find my brain today," he said.

He walked to the closet and pulled out boxes. He opened the largest ones first. He took out a stapler, a few pictures, some letters, a bag of old coins, and an empty bag of popcorn which he and his girlfriend, Kara, had shared on their first date. He looked at a picture of him and Kara standing in front of the fountain. He remembered every word said in that photograph:

"I'm not going to be here for too long," she said.

"Where are you going?"

"Taking a break," she said.

"From work? You can have my job. Being a clown is taking its toll."

"Let's take a picture in front of the fountain."

Abhra put the photograph back into the box. He went through the rest of the boxes and didn't find what he was looking for. He went to the living room and looked underneath the couch and the coffee table. He moved the cushions aside, but he didn't see anything. In the kitchen, it wasn't behind the refrigerator or in the cupboards or in the sink. The phone rang again.

"It's Bhushan."

"You're at work?" Abhra said.

"I'm about to take my lunch break. Come join me."

"Busy today."

"Busy? College is out for the summer, and you got the day off today. You should be clowning around, not being a clown."

"I have to find my brain."

"Are you drunk?"

"I've lost my mind," Abhra said.

"Is the whole Kara thing bothering you again? I know it's been rough on you, but it's been over a year now. It wasn't anyone's fault. She didn't tell anyone about her tumor, not even her parents. Nothing could have been done."

"I should have been there. Didn't even get a chance to say bye, and it's killing me."

"You can't do this to yourself anymore."

"That's why I have to find my brain."

"Do you need some help or something?"

"I'll give you a call later."

Abhra covered his face in white paint. He drew large purple circles on each cheek and colored them in. He put on a squishy red ball over his nose. He put on a bright yellow jumpsuit with green polka dots, and purposefully tied a necktie the wrong way. He tied the laces of his banana shaped black shoes and walked outside and lit a cigarette. The humidity made the smoke stagnant, hovering around his head. He looked at the tree outside of his house—its leaves speckled in yellow.

"Where should I go first?" he said.

He walked towards the market, looking at everyone as they walked by. Some wore business suits, talking on their cell phones. Others walked their dogs. Some walked like they wanted to run, and some walked like they had nowhere to be. The sidewalks smelled of stale banana peels and vinegar. He saw a couple holding hands and laughing. It was all one big circus to him, and he was the only one without a red balloon. He lit another cigarette and looked at the smoke traveling upwards and blending in with the gray sky. He pointed at a cloud.

"A brain in the sky. Where's my mind?"

He walked into the bank—it was empty, so he was able to walk straight to the teller, who was reading the newspaper. She had long black hair and black eyes. Her pointy nose was perpendicular to the counter, as her head was tilted to read the paper. Abhra sneezed. The teller looked up.

"Please tell me that you're just a clown, and not a clown who robs banks," the teller said.

"I'm neither," Abhra said. "I need to check my safe deposit box."

He gave the teller his information and followed her into a narrow hallway which led to a narrow chamber, where the safe deposit boxes were kept. He opened his box, MM1, and there was nothing inside. On his way out, the teller asked him if everything was okay.

"It's empty. Just like my head."

Abhra walked into a law office. He looked around the room and was going to walk back outside, but the receptionist asked if she could help.

"I've lost my mind," Abhra said.

"I believe you," the receptionist said.

"Do you know where it is? Have you seen my brain?"

A man in a suit walked into the lobby.

"Can I help you," he asked.

"He's looking for his brain," the receptionist said.

"I can see that," the man said.

"Do you know where it is?" Abhra said.

"Sir, I'm going to have to ask you to leave," the man said. "This is kind of weird. Please leave or I'll have to call the police."

"No need to call them," Abhra said. "I'm going to look for it there too."

"Jisha," Ty said. "Give the man a key chain."

The receptionist handed Abhra a key chain with the law firm's logo on it—a picture of an owl sitting in a courtroom, wearing a black robe and holding a gavel. Abhra rattled the key chain and gave it back to the receptionist.

"Thanks, but that's not it."

"Do something funny," the man said.

Abhra sneezed. Both the man and the receptionist laughed.

"I have allergies," Abhra said.

He went to the police department and walked through the security check. Nothing beeped.

"Figures," Abhra said.

A police officer stood at the front desk.

"Can I help you," he asked.

"Looking for my brain."

"Sir, have you been drinking?"

"Not yet."

"I suggest that you leave."

"Is there a lost and found or anything here?"

"Due to security reasons, I can't let you walk around like this. Come back when you're dressed properly and less threatening. Or less awkward."

"I understand," Abhra said. "I've lost my mind."

"I can see that," the police officer said.

Abhra walked into the drugstore. Virisha, wearing a knee length skirt with a button up blue shirt, saw him walking in. Her brown eyes and dark red hair that ended just below her ear lobes always attracted Abhra's attention. He was usually the one to say hi to her first, but he didn't notice her this time.

"Hey Abhra, what do you need today?"

"I'm looking for my brain," he said.

"You might want to try the cemetery—there are a lot of lost minds there."

"Thanks."

"Good luck."

It started to drizzle. The brains are crying, Abhra thought. Where could you be?

At the graveyard, Abhra picked a handful of red roses from a bush growing in the entrance way just before the black gates, then walked through the rows, eyes mostly closed with his arms sticking out before him—as he used to walk through the uncut fields to find the perfect spot to sleep. He passed the dead on each side of him, until he got to the last row.

KARA KITTUR, 1992-2016

He knelt down and put the flowers on her grave.

"I got you some flowers," he said, then sat and lit a cigarette.

After a few drags, Abhra put out the cigarette and placed it in his pocket. He sat on the ground with his back leaning against Kara.

"Lonely," he said. "My head is buried, and I can't find a shovel."

The drizzling stopped. He blinked his eyes four times and saw a human-sized duck.

"Quack."

"Kara?" Abhra said.

"You look so sad."

"Who are you?"

"I feel your pain," the duck said. "I'm drenched in sweat in this costume. Just a few more hours, and then I'm done for the day."

"I can't find my brain."

"Take mine," the duck said.

"Do I know you?"

"I'm Pival."

She took off her duck headpiece and handed it to Abhra. I'm working at the Children's Museum. I see you every now and then walking in your clown suit. What do you do?"

"I try to make people laugh?"

"Where?"

"Anywhere. I work for Chuckles—a company that is purely for making people laugh. At hospitals. At restaurants. Anywhere."

"That's kind of scary," Pival said.

"As opposed to walking around Kolkata in a giant duck costume."

"Quack," she said.

Abhra stood up and wiped the grass off his pants.

"So you go to the cemetery so you don't get too happy?"

"I've been looking for something. Thought maybe it would be here."

"Your brain, right?"

"You've seen it?"

"Not so much," she said. "Who's the grave?"

"We used to be together. She died of a tumor about a year ago."

"Where's your wig?"

"Don't know."

"Sorry to hear about Kara. Would you care to join me for some lunch? You look like you need a break or a drink or a break or something."

Sitting outside of a food hut, in the heat, the duck and clown ate their bhelpuri with sweat dripping down the sides of their heads and onto their necks. Mirages of puddles of water would come and go, and the earlier drizzling could be seen going back into the sky, forming a mist just above the road.

"Can't get over the death of the girlfriend?" Pival said.

"I don't know. I guess so. Since her death, I don't seem to have a brain. I'm motionless, thoughtless. It's taking its toll on my job. I can't smile. I can't laugh. I can't even cry. The other day I went to a birthday party—there was cake and games and a trampoline, yet I couldn't do anything to make them smile. Everything has lost its color."

"Maybe you need to take a break from everything."

As Abhra was about to reply, a boy ran up to him asking for a balloon. Abhra pulled a balloon out of his pocket, blew into it, and tied it into the shape of a dog. The boy's mother thanked him and they walked off.

"You're a celebrity," Pival said.

As he was about to take a sip of his drink, another kid ran up to him, asking him for a balloon. Then another child. And then another. Soon, Abhra was surrounded by a crowd of children and their parents, and he was performing for them with a napkin tucked into his shirt and spots of tamarind sauce on his face. Pival sat with the kids and watched. Every now and then she would turn to the children and start quacking, making them laugh. At the end of the performance, Abhra asked for a hug, and the children ran up and jumped on him, shouting, and laughing. Abhra fell to the ground as they all were on top of him giving him hugs. The parents pulled their children away, and Abhra stood up. Everyone was silent. Pival's mouth was open—her eyes were large and round.

"How did you do that?" one child said.

"What happened?" Abhra said.

"Your hair," Pival said.

"That's just the heat. It clumps up my hair. How bad is it?"

One of the mothers pulled out a compact mirror and handed it to Abhra. His hair was curly and fluffy and orange. It used to be straight and black.

"What happened?" Abhra said.

"You got your hair back," the same child said.

Abhra tried to pull out his hair, but it wouldn't move—it wasn't a wig, but attached to his head. The parents told their children that it was time to go, and they left, with their heads turned back, looking at Abhra, who was running his hand through his hair. One child remained, and she walked up to Abhra.

"Here," she said.

"What's your name?" Abhra said.

"Kara."

Abhra's eyes watered, the tears dripped down his face, causing the white paint to disappear. Kara put something in Abhra's hand and ran away. Abhra kept his hand closed.

"What did she give you?" Pival asked.

He opened his hand and saw popcorn kernel.

"Want it?" Abhra asked.

"I think it's for you," Pival said.

Abhra put it his mouth and moved it around with his tongue. He didn't eat it, but swallowed it whole.

"I found it."

"Your brain?"

"I just swallowed it. Look."

Abhra pointed at his own face.

"You're smiling," Pival said.

Abhra laughed. He laughed hard, so hard that his eyes watered and became red, like he was losing his breath. Pival patted him on the back.

"I should get back to work," she said.

"I'll walk with you," Abhra said.

"Quack," Pival said.

"I can feel again," Abhra said.

"How does it feel?"

"It feels like love."

The clown and the duck walked to the museum. Abhra got her phone number before leaving her at the museum to go home and change. His footsteps were in harmony with the thuds beating against his chest. He made sure to stop at the store to get some candy, and he laughed the whole way back to his house.

300 Rupees

We sat at Flurys, ate pastries, and sipped mango juice. My family and I were on a trip to Kolkata for the winter break to visit family and friends. This was my fifth trip to India, and I was enjoying it much more than my earlier visits. I was older than I was during my previous trips, and this allowed me to appreciate my homeland and learn things about my family history as well as my country's history. My parents and I had spent the day shopping after a couple of days of visiting cousins and close friends. We all needed to rest our feet from walking to several shops. The incense lit in most of the stores had made me dizzy, and the pastry store was a perfect place to rest. After my parents finished their teas, they decided to take a look at some of the surrounding shops to buy gifts for our friends back home in America. I told them I would remain in Flurys to either read or write while they shopped. When they were done, they would come back to get me, and we would go back to my grandfather's house for dinner.

Even though it was winter, it was still quite hot in India, and most of the shops kept their doors open. This brought in menacing mosquitoes. For some reason, I never saw them bother the Kolkatans, who seemed to have become like friends and neighbors to the insects. But mosquitoes knew I did not live in India, and wanted to taste my blood. Luckily, Flurys kept their doors closed, so they could not bite me. I pulled out my notepad and began to write some lines for a possible poem I wanted to give to my grandfather.

After a few scribbles a man came and sat at my table. This was common in Kolkata, as I was sure it was common in other big cities. When I was younger, it would really bother or scare me when strangers sat with me. But this time, I did not mind it. I nodded my head and smiled at the man, and he smiled back as he swirled the sugar and cream in his cup of tea. I continued to think of some more lines, but then I noticed that the man kept looking at me. He never seemed to move his eyes away from me. I looked at him again and noticed his aged features—the crinkles in his skin. The few teeth he had left were black and crooked, and his eyes were red and yellow. He had his gray hair slicked back, which revealed some scars on his forehead-they looked like burn marks. He wore torn sandals, and a brown t-shirt, which I assumed was originally white. He looked at my shoes and then my hair.

"Tom Cruise," he said. "Tom Cruise. You know?"

"No," I replied. "I don't know him. But I've seen him in a few movies."

"Tom Cruise. *Top Gun*."

"Yes," I replied. "That was a fun movie."

"*Top Gun*," he repeated. "You don't know Tom Cruise?"

I nodded my head. He looked at my shoes, then my hair, and then gave a big smile. He tilted his head towards me as I sipped my mango juice. I looked at the ceiling fan which moved slowly, but enough to circulate some air. I wiped the back of my neck with my napkin and thought about standing outside or moving to another seat. As I stood, he put his hand on my shoulder and I sat down again.

"*Top Gun*. Guns, missiles, everything. America is great, powerful."

"It's a nice country," I replied.

"President of the United States of America. President America. You know?"

"I don't know him personally."

"President of the United States of America. *Top Gun*."

"No. I don't think the President was in *Top Gun*."

"You want bomb?" he asked.

"Excuse me?"

"You want bomb. I give you bomb, missiles, anything you want. Tell President America, I give him explosives."

I looked around the store to make sure no one else heard what he was saying.

"No," I said. "He doesn't want any of that. I don't even know him."

I shut my notepad and put my pen in my pocket. The man was scaring me, so I stood up again and decided to wait for my parents outside the pastry store. He grabbed my arm before I could walk away.

"Tell Top Gun," he said. "I give him missiles. Very powerful. You take me there. I work there and I give him bomb. I leave here. Work in America for bomb."

"I can't do that," I replied.

"I good worker. Take me. I give you bombs and missiles. America great."

"Let go of my arm," I said. "Stop it."

He would not release his grasp. As I spoke louder and told the man to let me go, a small crowd formed around us to see what was happening. The man smiled and looked at the other people.

"Top Gun," he said. "President."

He began to chant.

"President Top Gun," he said. "Top Gun, America, Top Gun, America, Top Gun, America."

His chants became louder and louder. Then the man told everyone to leave and be quiet, and the crowd walked away. They carried on with either purchasing or eating pastries. He looked at my shoes and continued to smile.

"I go America," he said. "I Top Gun. I give missiles and bombs. You take me there. America great."

I saw my parents walk through the door. I pushed his arm off and began to walk away.

"300 Rupees for shoes," the man said. "300 Rupees for shoes."

"They're not for sale," I said. "I need them to walk."

The man smiled and nodded his head. He had a gleam in his eyes as he ran his hand through his oily gray hair.

"America," he said. "300 Rupees."

I walked out the door with my parents.

The Kolkata Bus Driver

The Kolkata mosquitoes fervently sought for blood in December as we walked across Park Street to find our car. They were stubborn and hungry. I thought I killed one as I smacked it on the back of my hand, but the mosquito buzzed around for a few more seconds and made another attempt. My family and I had been shopping the whole day, searching for gifts to bring back for our friends in the States. Shopping in the markets was quite tiring, especially when trying to shift about through the crowds. I could have worn a clown suit, and still people would have bumped into me and not realized that a clown had just walked by. In addition, once we arrived at a certain store in the market, we had to struggle and try to purchase our things at the cashier's while others pushed themselves into the queue. We would tell them to move to the back of the line, but most of the time they would not. Somehow, we'd managed to buy our items, such as a scarf or an ornament, but then we would have to go through the same annoyances during our visit to the next store. I was getting quite tired and dizzy, for each store had its own burning incense which would go straight to my head. The

93

huge crowds of people and the muggy evening pollution would strengthen my headaches.

By the time we finished shopping, I was ready to go home. Normally, when we needed to cross the busy Kolkata streets we would wait for as long as fifteen minutes to cross, for Kolkata drivers were crazy. Just as people did not see other people as they walked in the markets, drivers did not see pedestrians as they walk across streets. I believed that once they saw a pedestrian cross the street, they would even increase their speed to see how close they could get to the walker. I would have none of it though. I was ready to get back to the flat, so I could eat and go to sleep, for jetlag was still taking its toll on me. So I took one step onto the busy Park Street.

My mom kept calling me back and telling me to wait, but I did not feel like waiting for fifteen minutes just to cross the street. There was a short gap in between oncoming traffic, and I took another step. I grabbed my mother's arm with my right hand, and I raised my left hand to the traffic and signaled for them to slow down. My father was on the other side of my mother and took her right arm. Of course, the cars increased their speed instead of braking. I remained calm though, and kept my left hand up, and guided my mom across the street. She broke my grasp, though, and quickly jogged to the other side of the street with my father. But I walked. There was a public bus and a couple of cars headed towards me. I kept walking. My parents told me to hurry and cross the street, but I decided I did not want to. I was tired, but I was also tired of always being scared of the Kolkata drivers. They really did not have any respect for pedestrians. They thought they ruled the roads, and I finally disagreed.

As I slowly walked across the street, neither the cars nor the bus seemed to be slowing down. I kept my left hand raised and continued to walk at my own pace. My coolness began to change into nervousness, but I did not want to jog, run, or even walk at a faster pace than I usually walk. My obstinacy in such a situation must come from the Bengali in me.

I clenched every muscle that I could and readied myself for any hit, but I did not close my eyes. The two cars had passed by me, as I had already walked across the part of the street that they drove on, but the bus came to a squealing stop. I was sure that it would hit me, but it stopped and just grazed the side of my body. I heard both my parents scream and shout my name, but when they saw that the bus had stopped, they silenced their yells and quickly ran to me. The driver stepped out of the bus and walked towards me as well. He did not look pleased, and he began to shout at me in Bengali. I could make out a few words, but he spoke too fast, and I could not understand the bulk of what he was saying. By context, I knew he was mad at me, but I would have none of it. I started to shout back at him in English.

"What the hell are you doing?" I asked. "Don't you see me walking?"

He told me to speak in Bengali, and my parents were about to speak for me, but I told them that I would handle it.

"You're crazy," I shouted. "Crazy. You drivers just do whatever you want. Reckless and dangerous."

He continued to speak in Bengali. I caught a few words—words which meant "driving," "street," and "hit." I looked around and noticed a crowd had surrounded us. Some passengers from the bus stepped off and joined the scene. I could hear honking and shouting coming from cars behind the bus, but none of us felt rushed. I spoke in a firm voice, but I was not shouting anymore.

"Watch where you're going," I said. "You will kill someone."

I slapped the front of the bus with my hand, and then he slapped the front of the bus with his hand. He took out a brown rag and wiped it across his forehead. The driver was extremely skinny. He wore sandals, brown pants and a white button-up shirt which was stained with dirt. His unkempt hair must have been further mangled by the wind bursting through the bus windows as he drove at high speeds. Eventually, neither of us had anything else to say. We were both tired and angry, and we had both shouted everything we had on our minds. Finally, the driver turned around and walked back towards the door of the bus. The crowd had already lost interest and people went their separate ways to finish off their daily tasks. But before he entered the bus, he turned around and looked at me with the most confident of expressions. He lit a cigarette and then combed his tangled hair. He looked at me from shoe to head.

"You Americans cannot just act like you want here."

He spoke in English with a thin Bengali accent, but I heard him clearly. I was taken aback by his knowledge of English, for I assumed he did not speak any at all.

"What?" I asked.

He walked back into the bus, started the ignition, honked a couple of times, and continued to drive down the street. My mother grabbed me by the arm and guided me to the sidewalk where it was safe. My father looked at me and smiled. He put his hand on my shoulder.

"Now you've become a true Kolkatan," he said.

My mother did not seem too pleased about the whole situation and we continued to walk to our car. We were all silent during our trip back to the flat. At one of the traffic lights, as we waited and sweated in the Kolkata evening smog, a man walked from car to car selling books. He held about ten thick books in both his arms, but I could not make out what they were.

"OED," the vendor shouted. "OED."

"What is he selling?" I asked.

"Oxford English Dictionaries," my father replied.

Shome Dasgupta

The Author

Shome Dasgupta is a high school English teacher, living in Lafayette, LA. He is the author of *i am here And You Are Gone* (Winner Of The 2010 OW Press Fiction Chapbook Contest), and *The Seagull And The Urn* (HarperCollins India, 2013) which has been republished in the UK by Accent Press as *The Sea Singer* (2016). *Anklet and Other Stories* is his first collection of short stories. His writing has appeared in *Puerto Del Sol, New Orleans Review, NANO Fiction, Everyday Genius, Redivider, Magma Poetry*, and elsewhere.

His fiction has been selected to appear in *The &Now Awards 2: The Best Innovative Writing Anthology* (&Now Books, 2013). His work has been featured as a South Million Writers Award Notable Story, nominated for The Best Of The Net, and longlisted for the Wigleaf Top 50. His website can be found at *www.shomedome.com*.

The Author Thanks:

Mommy and Daddy and Deep, Heidi, Andy Breaux, Luke Sonnier, Stacey and Terry Grow, Rien Fertel, Katie and Denny Culbert, Bianca and Chad Cosby, Angelique Sonnier, Brandon Sonnier, Casae Hobbs, Lindsey Sonnier, Karl Schott, Eddie Barry, Anu Gupta, Jeff Distefano, Justin Bacqué, Tupac Shakur, Sara Ritchey, Leonard Chang, Jon Berthelot, Peter Manganello, Priya Doraswamy, Indira Kalyan Dutta, Rusty Nelson, Betsy and Neal Delmonico.

CPSIA information can be obtained
at www.ICGtesting.com
Printed in the USA
LVOW06s0851190517
534923LV00006B/26/P